Tiny Tim and Big Bertha:
Trouble With Jaws

Lori Milbrath

Balboa Press books may be ordered through booksellers or by contacting:

Balboa Press
A Division of Hay House
1663 Liberty Drive
Bloomington, IN 47403
www.balboapress.com
844-682-1282

ISBN: 979-8-7652-3333-7 (sc)
ISBN: 979-8-7652-3334-4 (e)

Library of Congress Control Number: 2022915439

Print information available on the last page.

Balboa Press rev. date: 08/16/2022

BALBOA.PRESS
A DIVISION OF HAY HOUSE

Tiny Tim and Big Bertha:
Trouble With Jaws

Tiny Tim and Big Bertha were happy with their family and home on the farm.

They had learned to survive and find food while constantly trying to avoid the farmer's cat, which the mice children had named Jaws. Tiny Tim and his family were always in search of food. They needed to eat and also store some away for the long winter months ahead.

Venturing out in the field near the farm, Theo, the oldest of the mice children, found something new. It looked like a metal cage. There was a raccoon inside of it.

"Oh, ya! I am so glad you came along," said the raccoon. "I am trapped in here with no way out. The farmer set this trap to catch animals that were eating his crops. Please help get me out of here before the farmer comes."

"I don't know if that is a good idea, "said Theo. "We are much smaller than you and are afraid you would hurt us, just like Jaws, if given the chance. That cat is always wanting to catch us."

"My name is Ricky," said the raccoon. "I just want to go back to my family. We roam around the farm at night looking for food ourselves, and we see that cat. If you help get me out of here, I will show you how this trap works. You can then use it to catch that cat instead."

The mice children talked together about what they should do. The idea of trapping Jaws was tempting, but dangerous. Theo was curious about the trap and wanted to know more. They decided to help the raccoon out so that Ricky in turn could help them.

The raccoon talked the mice children into pushing back the levers on both sides of the cage in order to release the door. The children had to brace themselves against the cage and push with all their might. It took a lot to unhook the lever, but they eventually freed the raccoon.

"Thank you! Thank you!" said Ricky. "I will help you reset the trap door, but you will have to find some food that the cat would want to eat. That will draw him into the trap."

Together they reset the trap and Ricky was on his way.

The mice children thought about hauling some of the cat's food over to the trap, but that would take most of the day.

At that moment the mice children turned around and saw Jaws looking right at them!! He was creeping along, ready to pounce! They quickly jumped down through the holes into the trap to get away from Jaws. They braced themselves against the back wall of the cage, as Jaws stood at the door. They were so afraid and didn't know what to do.

With a quick pounce, Jaws jumped into the cage towards the mice. At that moment the trap door swung shut and the mice children fell out the holes in the back of the cage. Jaws was trapped! The mice were free!

Of course, Jaws wasn't happy. He immediately wanted out. He growled at the mice. Theo, with his paws in his ears and his tongue out, teased Jaws a bit before they all ran home. The mice children told their parents what had happened.

The mice family worked swiftly to gather all the corn kernels they wanted from by the farmer's tractor. They were able to work quickly without having to worry about their safety.

As the mice finished up their work, they looked over and saw the farmer walking toward his trap to check it. They laughed as they saw the farmer standing there looking at the cat.

The mice were content that evening and prepared for winter. They also knew Jaws would not be happy to see them the next time.

Printed in the United States
by Baker & Taylor Publisher Services